Flip's Fantastic Journal

Me

Muzz

Mom

Digger

Sniffie

Ms. Flea-collar

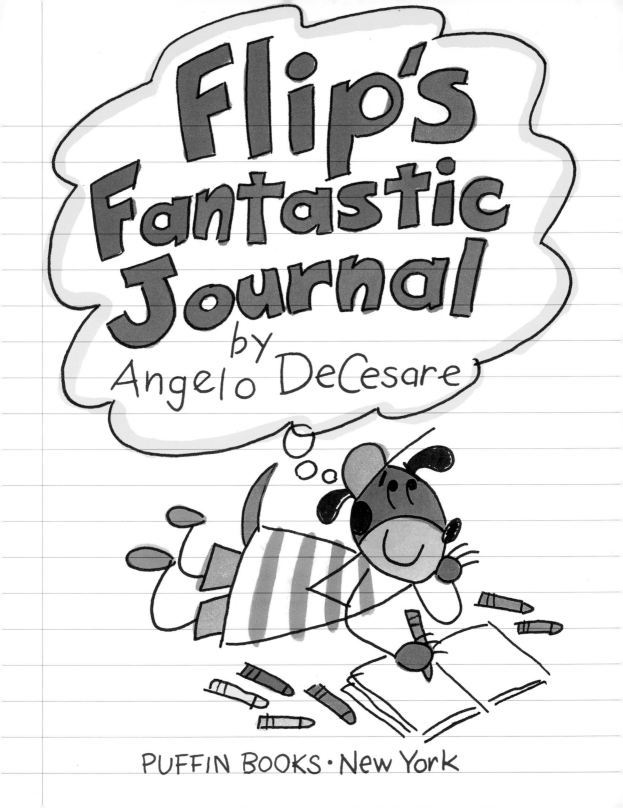

Flip's Fantastic Journal

by Angelo DeCesare

PUFFIN BOOKS · New York

Hi! My name is Flip. This is my journal. A journal is a book that you write in. You can draw in it too.

←Me

I like to draw. I like to play. I don't like to write.

This is my teacher. Her name is ⸂Ms. Flea-collar.⸃ She says that I have to write in my journal EVERY DAY!!

Please write in your journal every day.

I can write about things that happened to me. Or I can make things up.

I would like to make up that I don't have to write in a journal.

Today is <u>Friday</u>. I am writing about me. I live in a big building.

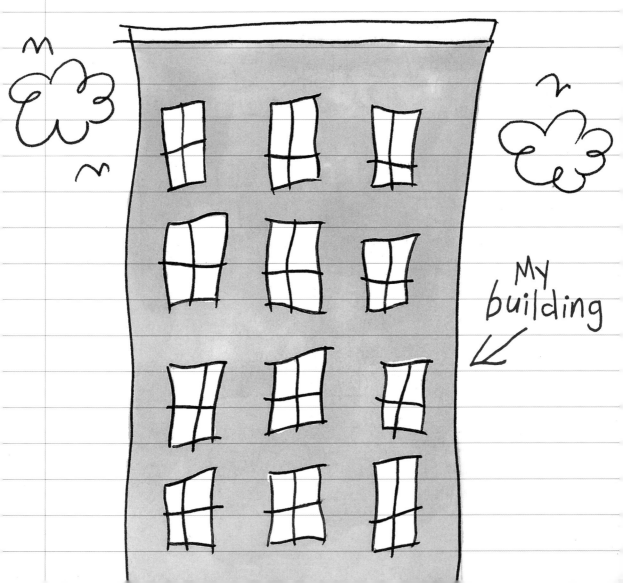

This is my mom. She
is nice. She doesn't
make me take a bath
every day.

This is my big sister
Sniffie. She is nice
too. Except when she
won't let me use her
skates. Or her radio.
Or her markers.
I changed my mind.
She is mean.

Now comes the best part. I have a friend. His name is Muzz.

Muzz is a great soccer player.

Muzz is cool.

Muzz is brave.

Muzz is strong.

And here he is.

← Muzz

That's all I can think of
today. Tomorrow there is no
school. But I still have to
write in my journal. Oh well.

Today is Saturday. Here is
what happened so far. Nothing.
But I will try to write about the
nothing that happened.

I didn't have to get up for
school. I was going to
  sleep ALL MORNING!

Except my sister wouldn't let me.

I had Yucky Ohs for breakfast. It's my favorite cereal. You get a free toy in every box. I tried to find the free toy.

I didn't find it.

After breakfast I called
my friend Muzz. I asked him
if he could play today. But
he had to watch his baby
brother, Digger.
I felt sad.

Then I got a great idea.
I would watch cartoons
on TV. I would watch
them all day. Without
even moving.

But my mom said it was a nice day. She told me to go outside and play. I said I had no one to play with. Mom said I DID SO have someone to play with.

My sister Sniffie!

My sister likes to race me to the playground. That's because she always wins.

My sister's friends were at
the playground. They did not
want to play with me. They
said I was too little.

So I kicked my soccer ball. I kicked it against the fence. Then it bounced back to me. Then it hit me on the head. Then I fell down.

I ~~swang~~
~~swinged~~ swung
on a swing by
myself. It
wasn't fun.

Then I found a piece
of chalk. I wrote my
name. I spelled it wrong.

Then I watched a bird.
I watched it for a long
time. Then it flew away.

After that I
went home with
Sniffie.

That's how I spent the morning. Doing nothing. Now I'm eating lunch. I am writing about doing nothing. I will call this The Nothing Journal.

I spilled soup on my journal.

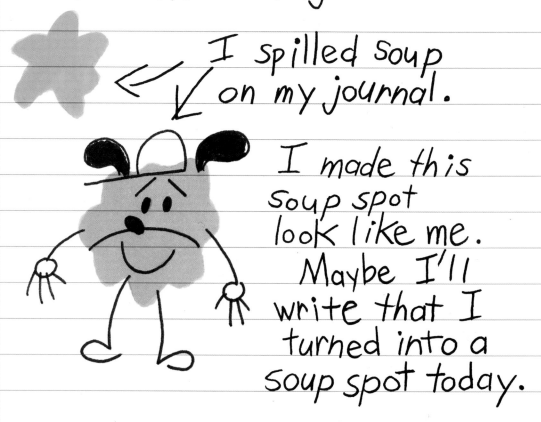

I made this soup spot look like me. Maybe I'll write that I turned into a soup spot today.

WOW! I just got a
GREAT IDEA!

I don't have to write
about my REAL day.
My teacher, Ms. Flea-collar,
said I can make things up.

I'm going to make my nothing day into a SOMETHING day. I will use my imagination. I will use my brain. I will use my sister's markers.

Presenting

Flip's

MAKE-BELIEVE Day →

Today there was no school. I stayed in bed ALL MORNING! My sister tried to wake me up.

I had Yucky Ohs for breakfast. There's a free toy in every box. Only MY box was FILLED with toys!

Then I called my friend
Muzz. He said he COULD
play with me today! He
didn't have to watch his
baby brother. His baby
brother could watch
himself. In the mirror.

My mom came looking for me. She wanted me to play with my sister. But they couldn't find me.

Then it was time to meet Muzz at the playground. I raced my sister there. This time I won. No contest.

My sister's friends were at the playground. They said I was too little to play with them.

But I'm not.

Then I saw Muzz.
We watched a bird
together. It
flew away.
So did we.

I got my soccer ball. I kicked it to the moon. Muzz said I was a good kicker!

Then Muzz wanted to go on the swings. But I knew the coolest ride of all.

A RAINBOW!
We all went for a slide. Even my sister. Even her friends. Now we're ALL friends!

Then I found a piece of
chalk. I wrote my name
on the WHOLE WORLD!
And I spelled it right!

Then I found a zillion dollars.
It didn't belong to anybody.
It was in my pocket. I used
it to buy lunch. I bought
candy, pizza and soda pop.

I shared my lunch with Muzz. We didn't even have to throw out the pizza boxes. Muzz's baby brother, Digger, ate them.

Today is <u>Monday</u>. I showed my journal to Ms. Flea-collar. She said it was great! And you know what? I can't wait to write in my journal again. Now I like to write.

<u>Wait</u>! That's not what I mean. ————————→

I LO
TO

The End.

PUFFIN BOOKS
Published by the Penguin Group
Penguin Putnam Books for Young Readers, 345 Hudson Street, New York, New York 10014, U.S.A.
Penguin Books Ltd, 27 Wrights Lane, London W8 5TZ, England
Penguin Books Australia Ltd, Ringwood, Victoria, Australia
Penguin Books Canada Ltd, 10 Alcorn Avenue, Toronto, Ontario, Canada M4V 3B2
Penguin Books (N.Z.) Ltd, 182-190 Wairau Road, Auckland 10, New Zealand

Penguin Books Ltd, Registered Offices: Harmondsworth, Middlesex, England

Published by Dutton Children's Books and Puffin Books,
members of Penguin Putnam Books for Young Readers, 1999

1 2 3 4 5 6 7 8 9 10

CIP data is available.

Dutton ISBN 0-525-46262-7
Puffin ISBN 0-14-056655-4

Printed in Hong Kong

the
author →

For my parents,
Vera and Michael,
and my sister
~~Sniffle~~ Martha,
with love.